THE
LITTLE TIME-KEEPER

THE
LITTLE TIME-KEEPER

poems by

Jon Silkin

W • W • NORTON & COMPANY • INC •
New York

Published simultaneously in Canada by George J. McLeod Limited,
Toronto. Printed in the United States of America.

First American Edition 1977

First published in the UK 1976
by the Mid Northumberland Arts Group, Wansbeck House,
Wansbeck Square, Ashington, Northumberland
in association with Carcanet Press Limited,
330-332 Corn Exchange Buildings, Manchester M4 3BG

Library of Congress Cataloging in Publication Data

Silkin, Jon.
    The little time-keeper.

    I. Title.
PR6037.I5L5   821'.9'14   77-21668
ISBN 0-393-04486-6
ISBN 0-393-04492-0 pbk.

1 2 3 4 5 6 7 8 9 0

CONTENTS

NOTE TO *HONEY AND TOBACCO*, page 23

For Australian readers, the few factual references may seem patronising. When the white men landed on the Austral continent they met with Aborigines. Whether or not the land is now shared, it is viewed very differently by black and white man. The poem attempts a bi-partisan view. The first section offers an Aboriginal view—of the flat unchanging earth. The last section collides the white man's round view, and its associated ideas of progress, with the black man's flat unchanging version of the earth. Section two names *Camden*, *Calvert* and *King*, a London firm which offered government the lowest tender for transporting the second (1790) shipment of convicts to Australia. Since in the contract no stipulation was made by government that the convicts should be delivered alive, the transportation became murder.

The author makes grateful acknowledgement to the following, where some of these poems first appeared: the Arts Council (*New Poetry I, II*), *Agenda*, *Europa Litteraria* (Italy), *Four Zoas* (US), *Jewish Chronicle*, *The Milton Celebrations*, *Meanjin* (Australia), *Meridian*, *Minnesota Review*, *New Statesman*, *Poetry & Audience* (Leeds), *Poetry North East*, *The Shakespeare Celebrations*, *Southern Poetry Review* (US), *Stand*, *Sydney Morning Herald*, *The Age* (Australia), *The Blacksmith* (Australia), *Times Literary Supplement*, *Threshold* (Belfast), *Tribune*, *Canberra Poetry*, and the Keepsake and Sceptre Presses. The author wishes to acknowledge Tyne Tees Television, and the BBC, in particular for the broadcasting of most of the group 'The Little Time-keeper'.

The author gladly acknowledges his debt to Charles P. Mountford for his book *Winbaraku and the Myth of Jarapiri* (1968) and in particular for 'The Creation of Winbaraku', chapter 2.

GIFTS AGAINST TIME
—Ella Pybus

1
On the insufferable flesh
over the creeping haulms, light

gauzes with saffron; and the limping soma
yields its psyche. The petite desert woman
crouches;
death's parched foetus.

Vulnerable hand-maiden, stay.

2
Who stays? In abundance
torches of sable light, in pustules soot
on the dump of after-life.

The livid melancholy of fat.
Extinguish
the greasy flambeaux, death stays.

3
Spiritual contusions:

serpent of roots, whose stung shape
writhes upon the earth lashing
with the prowess of miracles.

Be Moses: throw light on the wriggling bronze
over rock divine with water;
get memory quick with pictures
for our aching forms. I take

responsibility for
the fleshy images
I bring with me past death.

FOUR POEMS,
ONE NORTHUMBRIAN,
AND THREE OF THE HEBRIDES

BORROWING LIGHT

Earth, borrower of light. The rural institute's
fly-blown low-watt bulb spots the congregation
no root
for them. Tedium of earth, frustration
of bitter dahlias. Milk's sour breath deforms
by day the meadow's rim, the night's tense pupillage.
Their fly-blown memory is a lighted corm.
       Donor of light. Rank silage
laces the voids, shoe seizes its numbed foot.
Milk runs udderless, and the dawn defines
spillage of light, with frost ferned over cold soot
as bird-like sleep wakes in the long beams of the mind
its darker life folded in consciousness.
Prophecy is an ear coiling on entropy,
a bird receiving news with a thin lilac cry
rankled and stained by the physicist's black fly:
truth grooms with listless hands its darkening stuff.

IN THE PLACE OF ABSENCE

Winter's burnt light. Islands of stunned hills
in Gaelic smokiness; the calvinist spills
a bony lava of ill-natured prayers.

God of voids hanging in silence; human years
sweat and distill; an oaten sustenance
mottles with earth as memory despairs.

No leavening weight, of sand or flocculence
to make the peat bear up the jointed barley's light
spiked granary of demands, no long-thighed elegance

rustles the nerve. Libations of potash; grain
the fibrous mind to dust it has been led to feign
expectation of. Harvest's undulation

silk fish sprawl the quay, stars forge the night again
whose exile's passage tilths the screwed milk of the sea.
Lift up the veined bay in lamentation

in consciousness; it's grief distaffs the hair, mother
of sons. Squid sea, marble and indigo
of loneliness. The town's plantation sows

magnification of pain. Huge elisions pass
through the eye-rimmed sea.

THE HUNGERS OF COMMERCE

A minister's watch-chain hugs the cloth's paunched grain.

Where the wing rises to the gun, by harsh decoy,
an income is stuffed, like a spiked ear of rye.
The spirit's mash distills
the visitor's mind, ghostly and lyrical.

Raise up the kneeling deer. Bewitch the seas, and hoy
fish off their winged nets; the hotel's stormy pots
tint with salt blood of fishermen, that spilled
like lentils, like crabs and prawn mashed in the sty
of watery commerce
under the moon's tug, on the belly's tide
the wave's considered battering;
obstreperous needles stitch the tweed seas brushing Skye.

WEIGHING OUT LOSS

Fortune weights
to earth two heads, coppery
ill-luck

on lilac hills.
I hug the sacked peats I'll
lift

humped
to Lewis's malicious pibroch. It
opens Seaforth, first

of the earth, onto
Monsterless broken seas:
the Hebrides.

My tongue names what's
a whole lack

the supple magnetisms
of the thigh: to whom, to whom but
wind could I

offer my stunned prophecies?
Down the gangway bent the foot's
emigrations my

body cast
off its shades, and bespoke my drunk
phoenix exiled,

on the boat, of loneliness:
in the dense estate of the Glasgow
plantations

blood's the slighter tie of warmth.
As at the first, was

I done for in the plummet isles.

AUSTRALIAN POEMS

TOLSTOY'S BROTHER PLANTS A GREEN STICK IN THEIR ESTATE AT YASNAYA POLYANA. IT HAS HAPPENED BEFORE.

Sydney 1974

The woods at Yasnaya Polyana.

Eyeless leaves
rustle their neighbours' faces. Sough.
Sough: the wind. Tolstoy's brother
plants his green stick.

'If ever you find
this carved secret, Earth
will have greened a Paradise.'

Green, green.

Black men, abiding their wilderness,
scorch the defoliated, wriggling grub.

Whitely the ferry chunters us
between bays. In oiled dispersions
of wateriness we sprinkle to our rest.

The cut religious stick fades
among first plantations. Wind heaves.
Wordlessly, it vanished, bearing
what the hand gave, of brief warmth.

O supple Paradise. Integument
prime as our mother's breasts
folding milk.

The pouched marsupial intelligence,
its care, its teeth, stained with grass,
its leap to the peaceable kingdom, that,
that and no other thing, where is it?

The greening of a cut, wordless
Australasian stick. Wind lifts
like a huge leaf. Lovely questions
foliate the Pacific.

JARAPIRI
Sydney 1974

1

Mamu-boijunda: the spider cries
from below ground, Boohë, raising
life through earth.

Wanbanbiris, people of wood-gall
Latalpa, snake, and the death-adder Wala Wala women
blind husband-snake Jarapiri Bomba.
Wife Jambali, tugging her sons.
Each to the haired spider's word.
Scorpion Garangara pincers his itching prongs.
Our pleated feet cling
to the centipede, Jirindji.

Spider re-enters earth. Splintered
shale his legs, excreta
soft round stone in a heap.

2

Grass rests the two women, by whom
fire, lapping twigs; the waterhole flares.

Graspable, Jarapiri lies, huge
and toxic. Wanting him, they creep
through dried grass, like mice.

Jarapiri listens
to what is heard:
dry grass fastens to him.

No, no, he cries. No,
coiling himself,
his length fanged.

3
Jarapiri Bomba, blind, created blind.

What can an eyeless snake? The eye
attends to the dancing with voices tuned
for life's increase. So be it. Bestirs, coils
slithers to the dressed plain, where flesh
supplicates. Blind, but not deaf.

Can keep step, but cannot keep place;
trips, throws each dancer. Blind Jarapiri.

You fracture
our dance. Quietly, we
steal our life from you, since no entreaty
begs you home.

Wives, children, praise wetting their lips, all
evacuate the plain. Heat
of fire shimmers the vanished feet.

Silence calls out.

I die of loneliness.

4
We grasp our journey and walk. Jukalpi
the hare-wallaby, the egg-swollen women;
Lice drip from the wood-gall.

Haunted by two women, Jarapiri
will you coil and sulk? 'Old creature,
we'll hale you by the head.' So say
each of the sons, raising him. Jarapiri
lifts his wife.

5

How else divine how sand-hills, and the snaking creaks,
otherwise became? The sand plains
'clothed with eucalypts, spinifex
and the desert oak.' In nakedness
we make friends with an odd-faced land. The tale
unfolds at a touch.

Strange nocturnals gather the air.
The little birds shriek from their branches.

6

Poxed with beasts, the white schoonering men
unlimb our myths.
We have no figures for this.

HONEY AND TOBACCO

Sydney 1974—Newcastle 1976

1

A flat disc of earth. Light, dripping
work, the sun burrows through tired ground;
travels by night through musk
of she-fern, ochre, milk-stone, and oozes
on the cavern's face black light.

The Rainbow Spirit coils there
harder than the baler shell. Be still.

The moon gets up, and the Saucepan
pours out black milk
from which stingrays, turtles
and fish—quick, tomorrow finds them.
The spirit child chooses, swells
the woman, whose pain scatters
armsful of sparks frost hardens.
The spider Mamu-boijunda, upon
two hands: cries like an owl.

Honey and tobacco: the good and bad meet
and our child thuds at its opening. Croo,
croo fans the spider's howl. Sun
raises herself. Quick, where
male fern and woman fern spore in dew,
gather dew's liquid in sweep of the bowl.
Water for the child, and woman, quick.
We tread north between tree-ferns.
Our forefather's spirits, painted
in the same rock, get praised
and kept in their place. Shark, turtle,
Sustain us at the sea's edge. The disc
slops in its compass. No change;
the Dreamtime, perfect time of our Creators,
touches us, moves from us

2

1790. A year of conviction
for two apples, bruising the hold
the lowest bid contracted.

Calvert, Camden, King: onlie begetter
of us thousand fleet-winded
by our dear Lord's grace,

the tracks are Cooke's. Sydney's shore
inlays with brine, and the soft
judicious sandstone heat chews.

Wait. A hundred as good as dead
from food or its want. Stench
waylays the jagged rat: feed on us.

I touch our child, where nothing was
is something. Your flesh is coral
live with sweat, the sweet honeycombs

the strong. *Calvert* and *King*
paid to transport us, was *Camden*
bought to deliver us?

Save us, we beg: curved through
our flesh is the Earth's
fear at our axis. Listen

the prow's hiss subdues; Mary, hold
your milk to you, our child
is dead. Two-fifty dead

is the makings quarter us. Raise
us to the earth. Three

salt canvasses of their charge
wilt at their poles—a withered heap.

Off the shore, Commerce
evicts our dead.

3. *Mary is told Population is riches*

Property is theft; but some theft,
some taking back of earth's property . . .

the aching human form turns
through its flesh 'to God'. Ah
for such honey we dance
backwards who for our country probe
the sweet from the bitter. Gold

in England's Austral sun, our labour
combs another's sweetness; the grub
half-starves amidst honey.

Property is riches; what
is more property? When the white ships knocked
upon sandstone, all was poor.
'Copulate,' they said
opening the iron from us:
the rhyme breaks.

Fireside of the cove. Men fight
for us, women
suckling with gin the infant
desire for men's one possession, Woman. Begin
then we cried. The women
derived rum from the ships' masters,
feeding that, then their thighs; and withal
we come to it. Fire blows dew
off stone, this early day.

A kangaroo leaps
in its distance.

4. *The wanting*

Will we have a child, Tom, a second child?

My breasts so tendered with milk that touched
they'd burst. I am marsupial
and our child's mislaid in my belly. Find me.

Three-masted schooners stiff with drink,
their twanged rigging's the tarred voice
of Port Jackson. Even such music conceives.

Let her manage. My breath comes salt,
my soul's vapour on the quay grits
of crystal the sweated workshoe scrapes.
Drowned again, be under no man's foot,
I'd breathe my salt contagions through their flesh.

The thefted pastures lie
fat with the lambs of God.

The little birds shriek from their branches.

I thank God and ever shall
it's the sheepe has paid for all.

5

Earth gives: and the fruitful sheep stuff
the grazier's eye; desert grudges
its spidery paths. As black men grimace

the white creature tilths his furrow. By water
fluffed wattle dots the air. Here the black
tears his portion: 'a white child

enters our woman, water laps up
the white man, and the shark eats.' Mary
with second child white as a plaited loaf.

Passion turns over the lovely earth,
and ships fleet under the arc whose steel
barters train for train. 'Grace us,' we ask,

'span us.' Surely. We sometimes ask for
sometimes desire the contrition grace nulls.
Who, us? In separate sentences

we moisten our breath with theirs. Whose
selves darken? the bay with sun splinters
and blessings of a kind glance the white man.

Is it our sullen-hung selves numb us?
The grinding wheel unrolls tracts
of the New Earth; with forked lamentation

scorpion and snake twitch their insulted
flesh from our rubbery mileage. Give me.
Give it me. The flat unchanging earth.

SOUTH AFRICA'S BIRD OF
PARADISE FLOWER
Sydney 1974

In flower it is an idea of self
as bird; two nacreous tapering ears.
Nothing tappers in them. No hammer and no drum.

The neck flexes. Its cerise bird's-head
gouts its juice. It colours cerise.

Its ears plume. The head is a lower jaw;
the upper beak, a spindle with blue flanges.
Why no matching? Five rivets stud
and pair this creature to its under-half.

It unfolds deception. Two plumes listen,
and a silent beak emits lucent gum.
In Africa the black skin is black.

Not two plumes now, but swells, and pricks
a further pair, a second violet beak:
two birds rejoice over one neck,

and the body replicates huge leaves.

So fine the mode of words is its ghost.

The flower is its first idea. Rammed with
so much of itself, it furthers other selves

that multiply. And will not take flight,
rooted in austere bright irruption.

THE EXCELLENCE OF AN ANIMAL

THE EXCELLENCE OF AN ANIMAL

A sombre cat outstares
mild food, and that absorbs
the tentative black cat.

Your cry—its calculating
delicate balance of abandon

connects: your jaw fangs
with milk white hairs.

All your excellence has left you.
That is not true. Footprints

tacky with life pursue
their owners. Winter noon

strikes through its brilliance.
You are a black leaf

the pavement steps over.
Maythorned or grimed the car's

grim elegance consumes
the road, with a barely

apprenticed transfiguration
of lust two people quench

in the gear's change. The straight
road hits you; his woman's

moist basis transfigures
the breast's fleshy compassion.

We prised open your mouth, and there,
a little drench of blood
between the tongue and the palate.

Cat. Cat. The small head
eats out sight, as winged fleas

quit their host: as sin drips
from our dead.

All creatures with their ghosts

in any form, bring
yourself free of the wheels

ALIVE

Up trots the cat, and on
the bed three spokes array
a rimless wheel; and if

your mother's gone, softly
the radials of her care
dispose you; it is hard

to sleep, and hard to abandon
the mind's lucidities
stained to its under-self.

What is it? Candlewick
in your hooked claws; sleep is
a snapping of night's threads.

A bird cries, and worn flesh
refreshes in worn sheets.
Embalmed by sleep, allowed

our life by it, your gaze
raises its agate qualmed
with milkiness and stares.

Impudent pissing cat,
licking its penis that
is a bud tapering,

a soft barbed thorn, you are
alive in forms that cram
their sustenance through you.

THE POLISH GIRL

The moon never
had amnion, but of parent
ripped

herself: your walls
chalk with pain. Nubile and single,
your face steel

and lightness.
Your father Polish, your mother
a space:

a waterfall
of hair is your roots. Bride
without groom

whose fingers 'd raise
bloom on your loosened thighs;
how should I know?

Your smile opens
care; though skeined with no groom
you shall

lust and
none of me suffers
your bloom.

The skin tells it: take
joy with thirsting. Skein

and braid water

and may the hands, may those
that braid the fall, probe, and be mobile
as the soft waters of Poland.

WE USE THE LANGUAGE

Paired leaves, sprinkled with rice
and a black mouth.

Nature's dish. Mamma, what
is it? On the thatches

smoke the Portuguese.

A scream in ashes, tumescence
of gnarled blood
resists the thorny insect.

Ash drips, a deliberate
smoky unmanning of body. Go by:

cradled in her open belly
the half-born child, its valve of breath
pulses with labour.

The word 'portuguese' in English
translates as 'ally'.

Blessèd language, O blessèd be it. Cover
the bits of flesh

bring within the ribs of your word

gently my dear father
my gracious Lord, with much tenderness.
Like a leaf.

AGAIN

Friend, the blackbirds words, they dart 'wheep-a-wheep,
    wheep' so high up
not sufficing.

We have not met still, aren't about to.

The word I can't say
is, the waste.

And I don't.
Why did we never meet? the right
word, placating pain. No:

but the word admitting
your grief was correct

therefore acceptable.

Dead within
your own hand.

No, it's not true;
not the wrong pain, not, either, the just pain.
The pain.

Through the space I will
not pass, a few words

unacceptable, unbidden.

Who is to come to you?

YES

Abundance hoped for of
the springs, off which the heart
glebes sharp, hard water. Breath
through a heartless earth comes
heathery, carbonic. Dress—
get dressed by nine; our car
flows to the Registry.

Few ceremonied words
civic and unchurched: two
breaths wrapped our single forms;
marriage's double yes
effective terse and ringed
is the bare copular
of two assents. Bare flower,
tough willing alpine plant,
I hope. Springs that withdrew
as if to heft a fresh
gout of pure water braid
and steer onto the plains
benignant and alive.

THE PLUM-TREE

Our grave spittle covers his face.
Afraid I insult my God
of my poems I'll say little.

We married in late winter.
Mild as a pear, whose succulence
lured its priest. Yes, I said,
I believe; and miracles
balanced on pumiced hands. My door
glided shut.

I speak of the six million
and do not shave; no iso-rhythmic
evennesses of mind temper
the blithe compliant ratchets of industry;
and for the earth I work off, I earn
how much? We consider, and feed
the excellence of three cats.
When the sun undoes its pure,
fierce hands, I talk with the plum-tree
in the dene where mild limestone
kneels to the ice-floe. The tree's
incipience of fruit makes plump
the maidenly flowers: to what is torn,
wrenched, shot, or beaten, it can bring
nothing.
The dene's light crumbles. Of no use
if beauty affirm the techniques
work anneals; and, what droops away
is beauty as consolation—in the flame
work is of cash drudged for.
Barren are the plum-tree's flowers
fleshed as they glisten.

TWO IMAGES OF CONTINUING TROUBLE

Fountains Abbey

'For Christ' the rose stone avers.
Chaos of snows. Poured milk
of disharmonious stars.

White thongs in white commandments.
Like masons we cross our roof
in fixed devotion; which is

prayers' idealogue, image
of man changed to his praying,
the abutment to God's fleet

northerly hail. Shepherds pray
God come in gentleness.
The Crook forms its own question.

And it is gone; leaves clog
the chiselled epitaph.
The Cause pleads for a wreck.

The vanished crown flows
in dull rose to the earth
and stone gives the shepherd

to the face of coal. Do prayers flock
and cringe in the flaked
snowy vortex? it's as,

my God, you said it would be.

A prayer cup

As if steel, but a silvery
tar creeps upon Isaac
in Abraham's hand. Our Bible

is clasped in darkness. And for wine
three inches of the blood
of six million. The cup

wells Hebrew, and my grandparents
have tracked their kind into
the lake over-flowing

our curious feet. I who write
a factious poem want the means
to bless a christian. Breath

from the two locomotives *Work*
and *Freedom* steams over
the numbered faces.

Arbeit macht frei ('Work makes freedom') mottoed the camp gates.

UNTITLED POEM

The perfume on your body, and the musk of it.
The second is on me, I smell the first
on you as a sign.

I wear the undelicate odour.

Shuffling through the city, my mildness deceit. Hungry
and light-headed with venom. The adder silks
to refuse bins.

Fastened to the street: the working men's hostel past
two bins. A man beat me to those. I was afraid,
and the pulps he left stayed unfingered.

I had not thought of you: timidly
I spent my pence. In a dormitory
my body covered my trousers.

Along your flesh drifts your hair, a tree bearing
concupiscence, and your smile shows.
This is enough almost.

Your arms are slim, your fingers' amazing strength.
The tree's whole self blurts through long hair.
It's not grief, not joy; saffron spills
milk on the road.

A friend working through television gave
me a brass thruppence;
I bought tea with it, bearing nausea.

In Jerusalem the hills, bare; soft-haired goats
made of teeth; all the shoots are champed.
Hunger drifts through plains, over the declivities
of London; delicate smoky flakes of it.

On the rock splinters cold air; a coward
felt another's bruises in his groin.
He fears the cold air, its true match. Love, I love you.
Can I mean more?

You smile among four friends; three of us speak
and you say nothing. It hurts; your speech
is a silent woman.

Each night the kicked man screams.
If I help you. If I can lift you. His stain
over stone is blue, feather light.

The feet of police emboss the sidewalk.
                                          Linked
by my penis, our child could grow.
                                    Fear
synchronises with us.

I enter you. Local as a root. I wait
for you to get your breath. We measure each other.

We are prepared, lassitude melts. The hair
is naked, the piled spaces of hunger, and I touch
our candour;

the flesh in abandon robes gently
the tenderness. The candle's flame curves
round its inner light.

Your hair is sea-weed. You smile monstrously.
Memory flushes me through.
Your salt skin rustles on me. Of love, this entirely
is not what we were taught.

Thin black coffee in a pan flicks
beads of heat. The flaking city mounds
stillness, and amiable sleep
spreads our flesh.

We will not last, love, as we are. Love,
I would have us stay, ever, like this.

My conscience, my fear, and our sex, stir.

WE WANT TO SURVIVE

Sundown. The candelabra branches
seven flames. Sabbath is a taper.

The half-world douses sundown's fiery
indignant moral forms. Although

(surely) earth at its poles, flattened
like an orange, where blenched winds

precipitate with no end—earth tires;
inside that night we are its fires.

Is it against fire that one prays
each seventh day? Is every prayer

subliminal with earthly fear?
It's dark and the candles spit lightly.

Like hotel functionaries we hiss
with insulted life, who shrink with fire.

The cantor vomits wax, grease flares
his eminence. Six days worldly fat

burn on the seventh's consuming thread;
is fire the meaning prayers endure?

Admit the mind through fire. Of no sex,
on the burnished silver flame assigns

as equal mild deliberate fire.
Look, Isaac; and do not touch.

Self makes its fire. Each outer flame
selves its next flame that bears a fire

gravid with inmost flame, no flame
that does not burn, is an unburning

43

inner moist wax light. I bring

my grandparents in an image in
inside the inmost flame. Old men,

someone's grandparents, though the sons
and their sons' sons are ash, someone,

some old man holding to the slack
rough skin of an old woman prodded

past child-bearing, some old men
are still grandparents. And they putter

their Hebrew as the cuffed wrist bares
and passes moist bread, that the hand

has blessed and split. Take it, Isaac,
since you know the language. The moth consumes,

and Hebrew prints the wings that sheet
in fire. An unburned darkish moist

prefiguring resumes the life
of memory that neither loves

nor does not, linked in dissolution
to what dissolves, but does not go.

Not just yet, Isaac; no, not yet.

THE LITTLE TIME-KEEPER

ENTROPY AT HARTBURN

Between the hoof's cleft loam squeezes;
so beasts enter night-fall. Steamy
presences; the dunged breaths falter.

Hartburn divides night on itself
with a shutter. 'Mildred clamp out the dark.' Cream lace
embroiders its holes.

The huge energies untwine, and stars
slither away on the braids. The wagging stems
of sex slather to inane fruitfulness.

Not a thing to comfort us. The holly's fruit
taps at the church's stained glass
where solstice clenches its day,

and small energies out-thorn, the profusion
of winter at mid-night.

THE HOLY ISLAND OF ST. AIDAN

Primitive light streaks the sky.

Lindisfarne: wreckers clang their matins
and shine the guided light; the sea gulps.

Dawn lowers its leaden rose, the negative
sinks in the developer's tray. If men
are pierced by want

Holiness conceives murder. Midsummer
storms the sea and the hulk under
the long shook rope of waves

surges on Northumbria's teeth.
Mortal things. The flop, the cracking of them. Day
wipes clean that slate. The mild castle,

church, priory laced in Ionan
leaf, chevron, and the stone grape
smile to the sea. Mortal things.

The moon in its system, the connections snapping.

RIGA, OR THE NORTH SEA'S BERWICK

Light fleeces the Tweed's mouth
where there's no work. At this solstice,
the sun opens its hands.

The relationships. Ah, we remember:
our monument fathers our founding prince;
rears his stallion, that the balls

hanging to it glare at the people.

In the nineteenth century they were cut off;
Edison lit his bulbs. The white swans
work in them the city's ordure

to a kidney of stone. The mouth open in pain,
the river messes the sea. Stars
quit their diurnal circuit.

Entropic: the sprung clockwork
runs from itself. The animal's
equipment's been soldered back.

AT NIGHTFALL

Night-fall unfastens the door, and the font
baptises the raw body; womb
and its flesh pule to each other.

The mother's milk: clear and sweet
dropping from the soft pointed opening.

It's the stars count, and they flee us
inundating their absences
with our terse lives. When we die
we are dead for ever.

It comes clear finally. The Milky Way
vents its glowing hugenesses over
what's not there. The galaxies
pour their milk away.

Nothing's going to last

the clear baptismal water, twice welcome,
like two good hands

like the olive with
its stone of oil.

SHADOWING

Upon one straight leg each steps up-hill and burgeons
through a year's ring;
their leafs breathe.

'Clothes'. No, not clothes.

Arboreal men, shadowed
by leaves, so

shadowing us
we sliced our flesh from their shades

that cut away, the trees lie
acquainted with the shadows of death:
for which there are words
and no language.

Give me your branches: the woodsman
handles their deaths: a blade and its haft.

Then us. Earth washes away. Leaf,
leaf leaf

like treeless birds

SHADES

Cheviot: makes silence of
life's bare soft maximum,

fluxing not much. No, hangs

its milky fluid in
Henhole's vacancy; plump

bellies of cinquefoil mixed
with the Barren Strawberry ooze

their lobed flesh at the cleft
Cheviot turns into;

and through the soft
crushed odours, what trees?

The Elderberry and
red-berried Ash, not here,

in the North's summer dense
with shades. Do they

grow in us; do our selves form
on theirs? The Oak's

rooted head branches joy
with leaves close as wood-grain

with between them birds
numerous as mustard grain.

Not here. And yet here, even
so, the passions of form.

I need you. Who else,
who else but you?

the huge strong soft presence
with roots; robust

musical presence

your shape
of noise ghostly

with permanence:
                    Tree.

THE MARCHES
For Isaac Rosenberg

the half used lives
lift in strong hands an image
of their blooded faces off the freshet's
watery layers

death's ill music creeps
its heathery silences
upon the ear's lulled smithy.

In silvery ounces the Rede
waters through wedged stones;

we are two
in the forest's numerology,

where the mouth casts up trees
numerals
the rip-saw chews;

papery type informs the novel's
symphonic lexes.

To write a poem
from which breathe
the silences.

FOR SOME TIME YET

Where Catcleugh soaks, turn
by ballistae pilfered. Dere Street

is running sprucely. Striae
of the North's Rome

where flesh blanches on the short sword.
Fleeting death
mouths peat and amnesia.

Like blood, the sharp wrens
drip from the hanging tree.

High Rochester, the square common
in fee to no-one. The sun
bathes in its gorgeous Sabbath.

The Sabbath dove puling in the wall.

The square's greening of the fort.

In the edgy grit springer and cap
groove a gate's masonry. Dere Street

leaps off the eye. Three staunch houses—
and the wall, staggers some yards: domesticity
dribbles to earth.

Sandy heat, and russet
hens in this place of white eggs.

Cluck. Warm comfortable upright
hugs the brood; their mush heaped.

Black agatey eye blent
with Sabbath's heat.

The sun's glance plucking time;
a hen pecking it.

JESMOND'S WELL

To give the water shape
as water forms us

at whose well-head, into
which water braids, *Gratia*,
is carved:

for this source, thanks; at which
to give it that we say

'St Mary's' where it comes
to light, pulsing over

the ground Quaker and Mason
have made a grid; a couth

grim elegance subsumed
by brick in plots. Water

streams a costlier fragrance, Earth
of the ratepayers. The principle:

stealth, care, interest

the flesh white as milk, charitable
as warm bread

CENTRE OF ABSENCE

Names for one street: Pandon?
The same course
winds hesitantly to decay.

Pampedon is *Pantheon*. The Roman site
opens a Greek name: *pantes theoi*
all the gods. Oh, yes;

the city will scrape this
from itself. Mender of graves and teeth.

Clop: the worthy feet counsel
speculative contracted powers.

Stars burn in the simple dark;
our dense lives fly.

First, Jew-gate: rain sluices silver
braiding usury on the stones

with workmanship. Newcastle buys
the Jews' expulsion. The King

is all gold; Judas bit small
in the coin's realm. So, the King's light

clatters upon the streets. 1656,
'Come in again,' Cromwell stutters.

Jew-gate, in traceries
of despair

the systemic fountains
of prayer and flesh

Trade's filigree rubbed
of instinct; the steep street

slithers through vetch and ground-ivy.

Over by the Quayside, as if a hanged man
cut to morsels, size of a dog's mouth,

nothing. Decayed commerce

transacts melancholic Scandinavia
in desultory amber beads. 'Ye divvent

knaa nowt heor.'

BREAKING US

1
Moss sprinkles its cry; in the bowed
fields of wheat, poppies
flutter themselves.

Love, come on.

We hand-cut stone fruit
in the lintel over the door.

Blessedness in that.

2
Turning its arms, the caterpillar flails bricks.

This section is almost ended.

Tears that would come
press back their springing.

A cry flutters on mudded tar, its road
a wheel that unrolls, hastening.

Street sellers of innocent fruit
are touched by the police.

The lintel with fruits, splits.

3
Smells of tea on the shut
curtains. Winter's light
puts its arms round the house.

Touch me, she says.

The rug at the fire, and the fire
warm us.

Love, our child conceives
amongst wool and the milled
white bread touching you.

4
So much spills. The look
you gave the house
goes down with it.

The wheel drives downhill, mudded
in under the Tyne. An oiled rag
stretches to brine.

Our house, love, done in.

Wind dusts dust with it.
Their plan unfolds in a flat way
a flat road, where the rug
laid our thighs.

There, dust off clay blows from
the despairing chimney breasts.
Nichts, love.

5
What we have been given.

Given? Brick for chalking on;

the rush through the eye
of the summerless high-rise,
each jot of dust rented.

Dust off the armaments
smokes into our heavens. Consecrate this
constructed at the rim
of the city's eye.

The cheerful councillor's face
gleams off the earth.

'All power to the constituent city assembly'

No tree, grass. The caress
of it at best the going
drab daily.

Love, we are dust, owing rent.

The rag stretches to the sea.

This section is also done with.

FIRST TO LAST

1
The Milky Way: a chart, a conducting
of white bodies
lit by time in darkness. Off

in another place, spirals of milk
curd that darkness. If we fell
to where would we fall? Prodigal forms

that pour away.

There's no grasping them: no name
reveals the parent

in heavenly nakedness.

2
Here sprouts Meldon: *Moel-Dun*,
a hill
shimmered by cross, by cross or sign:

to house, to haven; in 1242

the needful light.

Church as a long room, chancel and nave
one plain intrication. Snug house

a round low vault of stars
ceilings in blue crosses, blue and blood,
shadowed with gold.

Were we gentle, so would this be.

3
Traumas of smoky shadow.

Bolam: of two names one
forced on the other: swollen ground.

Creation names her groin.

But before this, where we cut
their shades from us, place of the tree-trunks.

The likely pastures char.

Sheared from Rome, the Causeway
runs off. Poind and his stony dog
mark the foot's emigrations

grass persists in. Mound and stone

ponder the North's shadows:
the acreage of green farmers
under huge leaves annihilating
in shade their greenest powers.

Amongst the tumulus the short
dolerite coffin, grained with soot
upon the lumpy

glutinous flesh. I can't say.

For what's there, what is it? eyelid
bereft of coin, no bones
tumbling through earth. The grave

envelops no name. Death
has burnt away.

And smoke, lingering.

WHAT CAN WE MEAN?

who didst stretch forth Thine arms upon the cross, to draw all
men to Thyself . . . give peace to all nations

The Flodden Prayer

1
The prompt field of battle

is a chart, on which
men deform each other

a well, course-pipe pulsing
its lush onto the soil.

2
A proud Prince, through England . . . a King
etched over Scotland: the drums throb
upon the furled heart's beating
in equal brotherhood of pain.

Blood paints blood; is this
to be human, above mouse, or the oiled
fur-clung otter? Flodden

notches the ranks, and the rank
is a gap in the tumbling line.

Cry, what shall I cry? Our flesh
is grass, a withering
its clause in the syntaxes.

Soil recovers its right mind
however heaped is ditch
of blood or burial;

the living are a wound one
upon the other. Sunk flesh
and the tried soul perish

one in the other. 'Flodden'

the mind bursting its soft
root of blood

3
He harries another. There breed
no wounds to the battle, none,
but the shared nuptials of death;

slowly haling the body
from itself, that bespeaks
its mutilations. Stop that.

Sopping the green worsted, blood
pulses on, whose bare pain
death shags many ways. Enough;

but pleasure's innerness, silence,
voices lust's fury, his body's
very breath. What does

it matter what we do
to our lives; the stars

will freeze their milks apart
in equilibrium.

The soul nourishes in blood.

4
It is the discipline
of strong men that clasp
the weak into strength's ring.

Clap your red hands, our pikes
devour their flesh; jawbone
brays in an ass's shape.

Were it in us to be
as God, and break his covenant,
we'd rive soul
to the spongy equivalence
of torn life. O, then,
by all means, purge and disperse
each nucleus as if
a blooded soul. Donor of light.

Life through our pikes, we cast
our arms wide.

THE CHURCH IS GETTING SHORT OF BREATH

Sabbaths of the pensive spread buttocks.

Conscience, the size of a dried pea,
chafes over the pews flesh sweating

its Sabbath juice.

Douser of burning wax: old man
hugs remorse like a first wife. What labour
will such bridal pains be fruitful with?

First night of marriage wakes the bride
to shimmering kindness; our hemisphere
dishes the Sabbath, dead prayers,

the dulled rose of texts, desert mica.
Air breeds to the shy nibbling tourist.
Work-day fingers the rosary of work-days.

Work's necessary bead; the mechanic
wrenches the thread by which our lives
fasten to us.

Coming first to church, sharp
as the warrior wren. Morning dews
the prompt mind, tourist of the holy
places pious with no use.

This is the true debating-ground,
and here the praying hands consume
the life they build. I shall do what I can,

The question loses its memory,
and the dense shade, in the spaces, runs
to hydrogen

laconic as its dull copulars.

Sneck the latch-door; Adam from sculpted
wood raises Eve with himself
to the bridal shapes. Love congregating

the bench will have its forked play
of their clasped forms: I have come to an end

of the ancient days. Laboured tweed
surplices the rich man.

My lovely parents, when you shaded
each in the other's thought, and flesh
pleaded one anatomy, of life,

endless life, death's frail nucleus
sweated to come alive, its soul
in our flesh. I loved my origins.

But you mid-wifed death. So I became
man, and as others judged me you
I judged. O gentle God, with both hands

you lathed prayer, a chariot's flange, God
of hope. The stars' system contracts,
that, or they flee us. Of such fountains

we lie in the solar ground, and the question
loses its mark.

LATE POEM

Cheviot's milky calm is summer's
dis-playing paradise. The hill

swells, and pouts until Henhole
opens, whose fluid strip

hangs in air, a gravity
out of nature. No trees;

its bare flesh grassed, stocks
the smells of a pharmacy.

Long gentle flesh, solstice
of deep hot contralto in the air.

Nature, in friendliness, gives

the crucial means stir.

Behind light, the darkness
to be believed, in which

sparse hydrogen

lethargic, as the mind
of a successful graduate.

Stars: the systemic fountains
of plural milk pour

away, not
for ever, to

dead equilibrium,
the system indifferent

as a dried hand. Here
was our flesh, and love
moistening itself that burgeons
perfect form as if

it could not go.

When we die, if we
are dead for ever, it must

be of no concern; the planets
will lie apart.

Thus the architectures, desponding
of joy; church, or the camp tower

nesting a vigilance of fire.

I think of light: vertigo
in light's dynamism as

it flushes between folded
hulls of concrete

through hidden glass, motioning

death's volition in me, and bellows
upon the concrete.

No, not that way, even
as architecture elegances
huge chill grace. Three things:

an inward clashing sound, as
of love; to have lived
is something. Equalities

of tenderness no thing smutches.
Sleep before two deaths, flesh
of despair, as the mind weeps

its disemployment. We smudge
the echoing humus: the stars'
heavenly system annuls.

We reach, we reach in

measureable loneliness

unless two shudder on the body's
richest extremity.

Fountains of prayer decease.

If the universe were stranger than it is we'd go mad. Flodden Field indicates Northumberland's role as the Poland, or marching-ground, of Anglo-Scottish relations. When there were no wars there were feuds, and with or without feuds were the moss-troopers and reavers. Cattle and horse stealing were a rule. After Flodden, while the English soldiers were stripping the Scottish dead of reparations, local people got into the Earl of Surrey's camp and lifted the growing plunder. The Northumbrians were more thorough than the Cumbrians, Cadwallader Bates suggests in his 'Flodden Field', and what better time than when arms were busy elsewhere. The English army was as moral as the Northumbrians, and if the latter were more devious, they had endured the trespass of too many armies to keep active a sensitised compunction; theft, they might have argued, cannot be made legal.

There are other ways of being provincial, and the collaborative root shared by Northumberland and my anxieties about space are here locally enacted. Even so, the root-expression is not a technical means for supplying the existential substance of an abstraction. The local is an exploration of becoming; it is a means to habitation. And for all that, Wordsworth's altered phrase evinces the connections without showing the needs of the anxiety. Thus I call the group 'The little Time-keeper' because that's how man works for his security—by computing his presence in relation to the planets' motions. The Aztecs got it to such a pitch that they could compute what day it was some two million years previous.

You can travel the area with Pevsner's and Richmond's *Northumberland*. Its compact 'history' provides a mind for the eyes, and the remainder of the book defines what the eyes see. Even so, there are the inevitable gaps—Middleton Hall, for instance, or the Meldon church's ceiling. Yet to mention these is to point away from the real gaps. Architecture may be social history but, one might ask, whose history is it? Pevsner answers that question when he writes of Wallington that it was a house 'built by Sir William Blackett in 1688 out of the proceeds of coal and lead mining, shipping, and Whig convictions.' That isn't all you need to know, but it's a great deal, and it compacts all that an account of the region's architecture must omit because it notes only the fine-looking, the worthy and the beautiful. Behind the beautiful stand the cooks, stone masons, and the brutally underpaid who worked the mines and shipyards. In this sense architecture is a social history in default of these. They are truly present: the house they built or paid for, with their labour, are more truly their monument, in more than one sense, than they are ever those of the Blacketts and Armstrongs. And if the Armstrongs, the Ridleys, and their peers had their house built, what did they 'build' for their workers? To discover this is not to read about the beautiful-as-the-leisured. It's to read pages of bland indignation, and these are texts the middle-classes will buy only if their professional occupations require it of them. These are the proprieties. And these are the deficiencies Pevsner's and Richmond's work entails, as it were, by definition, and it must therefore be a tribute to their work that such deficiences are so adequately delimited.

I find the other deficiency in myself. The fear of eternity started to grow in me when I was about eight. The fear isn't unique; writing in 1933 William Eddington noted:

It is true that the extrapolation foretells that the material universe will some day arrive at a state of dead sameness and so virtually come to an end; to my mind that is a rather happy avoidance of a nightmare of eternal repetition.

(*The Expanding Universe*, 1933, p.125)

The fear is made up of a crux. On the one hand there is the terror that after death 'One short sleep past, we wake eternally'. What in heaven could one do with such time? But if that is fearful, look the other way and perceive entropy. There, the fear is generated not out of traditional beliefs handed to one like some awful gift, but by that traditional substratum put under pressure by the new physics. And it's both problems that bind together the fear. My background is a mixture of rationalist agnosticism and dilute orthodox Judaism; the bases of my spiritual clichés are identifiable in the familiar approximation of anthropomorphised eternity. If I disposed of God as though the problem were intellectual, I also believed, in a childlike mode of half-assumption, that all I had to fear was death. When I died, my spirit, and perhaps some version of my flesh, would rest in eternity because, by definition, that was its provision. I could merge my existence, if that's the right word, in eternity in the way that a child merges its existence with its parents'.

In 1865 the French physicist Clausius reversed a crucial assumption about the nature of cosmic energy. Prior to his formulation it was believed that the energy deployed by the stars and their planets was limitless, and that therefore their life was as infinite as time. The stars' limitless energies and time's eternity were one.

Clausius formulated the idea of *Entropy* whereby the energy of the planetary systems is not limitless, but finite. Energy expends itself; it is self-consuming and not self-perpetuating. The universe, to use a perhaps misleading analogy, is like a clockwork motor and its impulse is finite; when the planetary energies are exhausted the heavenly bodies will lie apart in dead equilibrium. Energy is disequilibrium constantly if unevenly moving towards total expenditure and rest.

The analogy is negatively suggestive. The clockwork can be re-wound and set in further motion if, by implication, the hand of God is there to do it; what the system cannot do is re-wind itself. Clausius's formulation crucially effected the removal of physics from tacit co-operation with theology. Thus if energy does turn out to be limitless, and if the entropic view of the universe is at the same time correct, then it will be the hand of God and not physics that does the re-winding. The entropic view does not support the optimistic if terrifying belief in a cosmic eternity. On the contrary, if theology is committed to a prospect of eternity, it's a view it will have to advance without the aid of physics. Theology might reply that it has so far managed very adequately without it. Is it more adult to trust to faith or the new science?

74

BIRD

You flew into a rage
but against glass

your wing grasped its mistake
and broke. Wing and hand

in pure helplessness we step
through that oval, the eye's

thin stoic fluid.

Pitchblack
and dense

grows the flickering will to live.

Off the anaesthetist's slab,
the mortician of gas, hop

through the ranks
of men.

Your chirrup

all gold
on three toes. Black distinct intelligence,

from the mishap of gas, beat
through men's ranks

slewed
on Boxing Day.